My Friend Rabbit

ERIC ROHMANN

ROARING BROOK PRESS
New Milford, Connecticut

For Nicholas, Ethan, and William

Published by Roaring Brook Press, a division of Holtzbrinck Publishing Holdings Limited Partnership.
143 West Street, New Milford, Connecticut 06776

Library of Congress Cataloging-in-Publication Data Rohmann, Eric. My friend rabbit / by Eric Rohmann.—1st ed. p. cm. Summary: Something always seems to go wrong when Rabbit is around, but Mouse lets him play with his toy plane anyway because he is a good friend. [1. Friendship—Fiction. 2. Rabbits—Fiction. 3. Mice—Fiction.] I. Title. PZ7.R6413 My 2002 2002017764 [E]—dc21
ISBN 0-7613-1535-7 (trade edition) 10 9 8
ISBN 0-7613-2420-8 (library binding) 10 9 8 7 6 5 4 3
Printed in the United States of America First edition

My friend Rabbit means well.
But whatever he does,
wherever he goes,

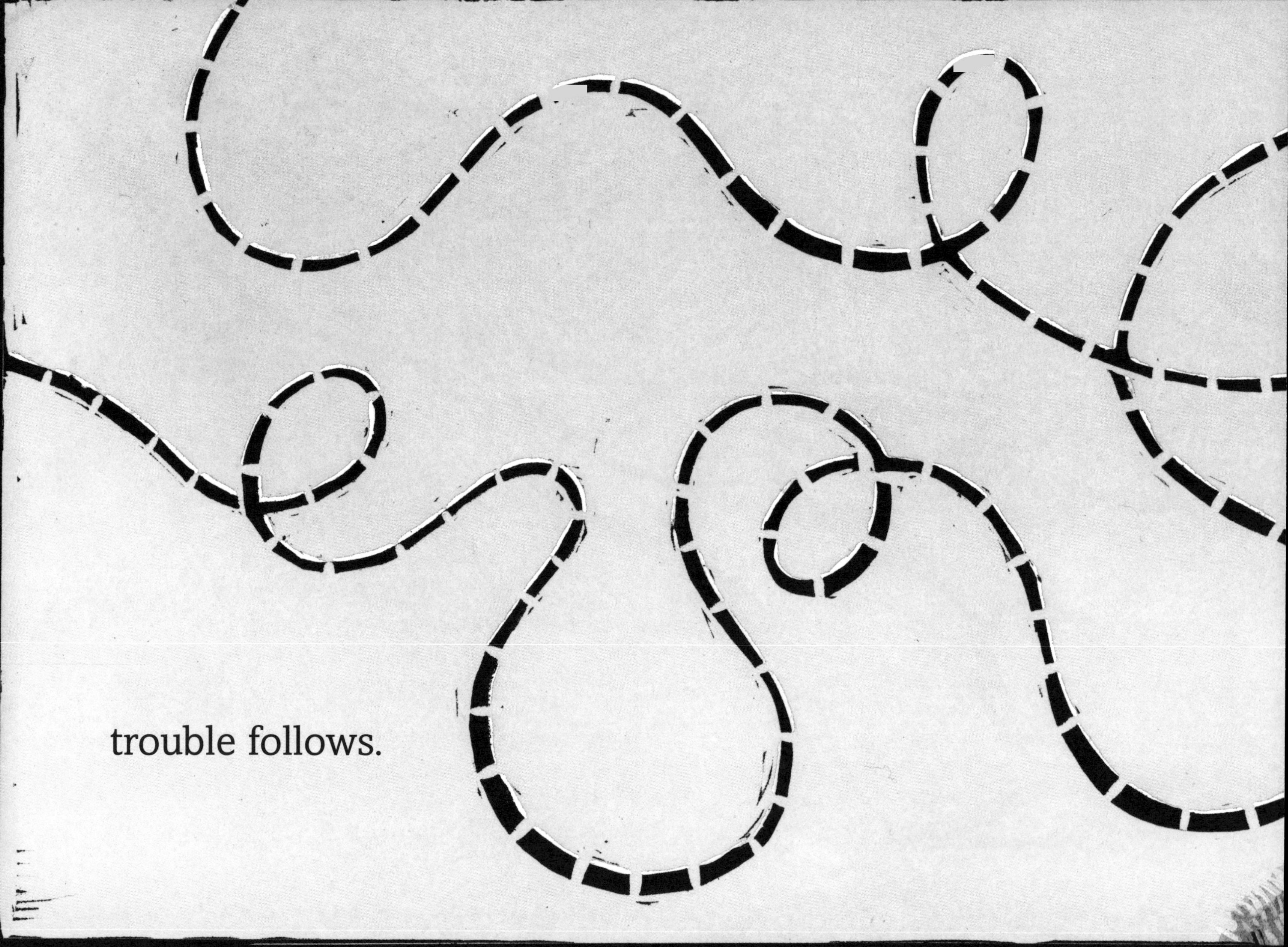

trouble follows.

“Not to worry, Mouse. I’ve got an idea!”

The plane was
just out of reach.
Rabbit said,
"Not to worry,
Mouse, I've
got an idea."

So Rabbit held Squirrel
and Squirrel held me . . .

but then . . .

The animals
were not
happy.

But Rabbit means well.

And he is my friend.

Even if, whatever he does,

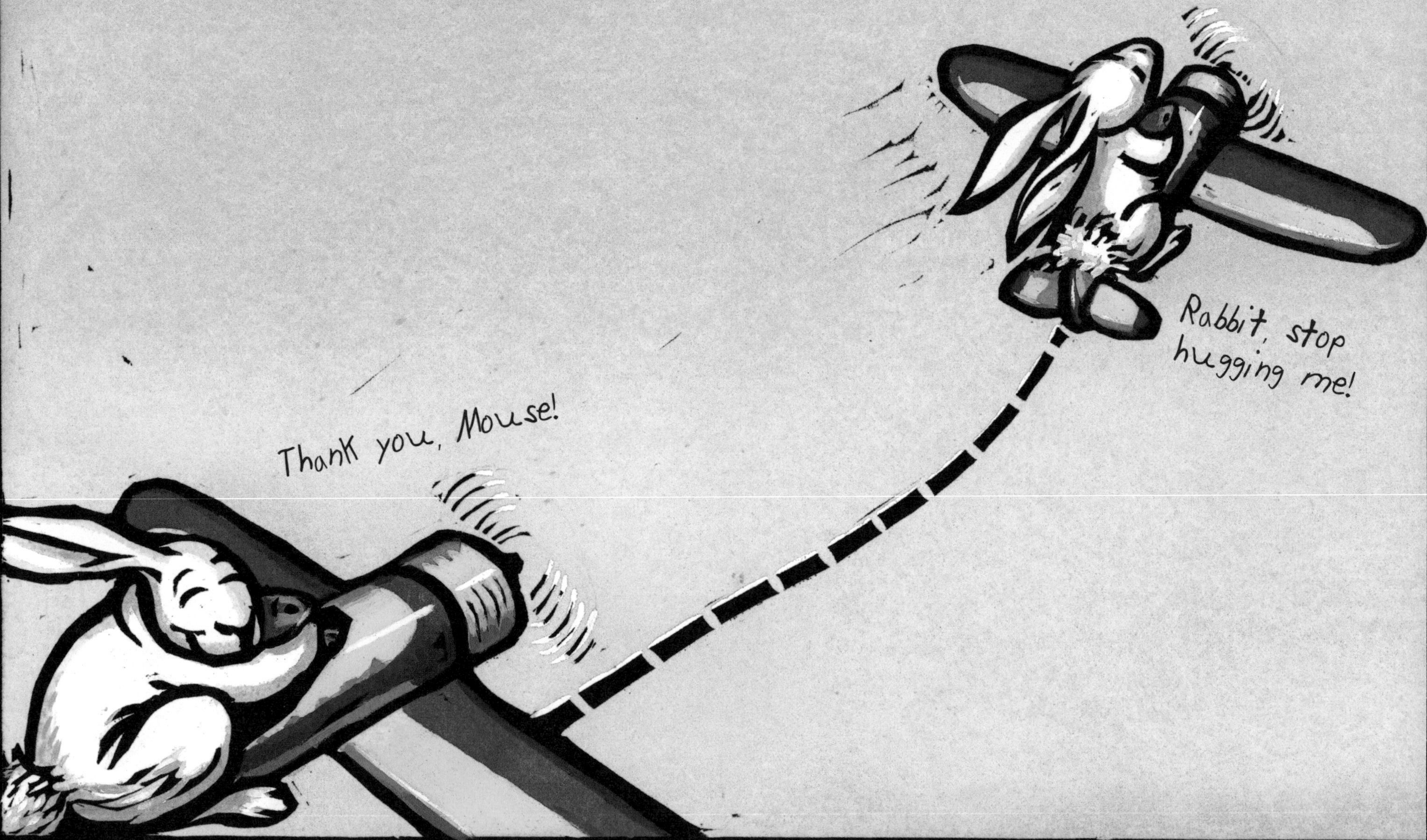

wherever he goes, trouble follows.

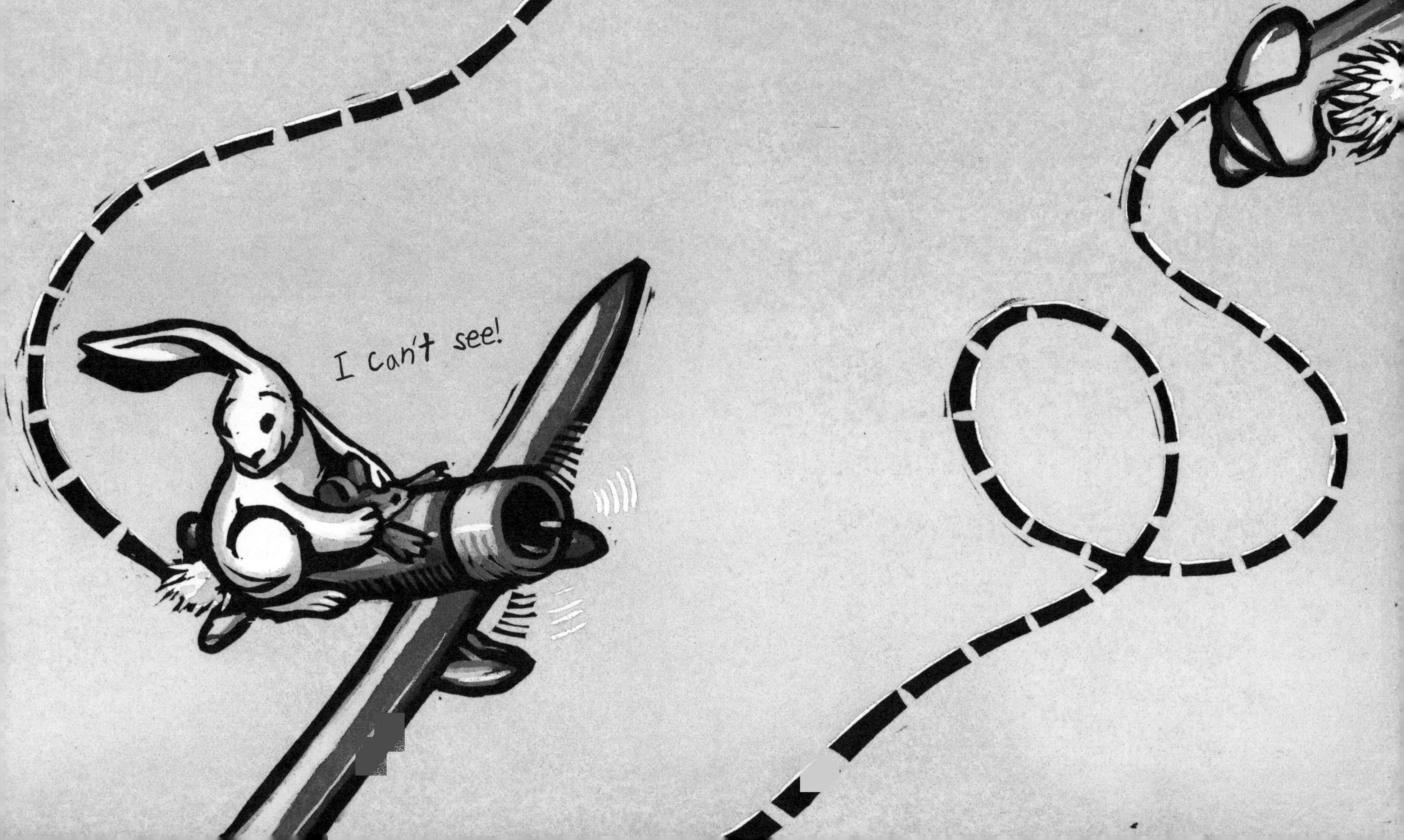

"Not to worry, Mouse,
I've got an idea."